Love & Lies in Snow Valley

Desmond Hooper and Kendall Shelton

Published by KMDA Signature, 2025.

LOVE & LIES IN SNOW VALLEY

First edition. March 24, 2025.

Copyright © 2025 Desmond Hooper and Kendall Shelton.

ISBN: 979-8993284507

Written by Desmond Hooper and Kendall Shelton.

Love & Lies in Snow Valley
by
Kendall Shelton & Desmond Hooper

This story begins on a frosty evening in a small town in a valley surrounded by snowy mountains. The streets are quiet except for footsteps crunching in the snow. Two strangers are about to cross paths, and their lives will never be the same.

The woman's name is Madalyn, a small-town girl who still lives in the house her parents once owned. She runs a pastry shop that has become a town staple.

Opposite of Madalyn was Jamie. Jamie did not like the snow, let alone the cold, and was a traveler with roots in the Sunshine State of Florida. As they tattooed their footprints in the snow, each absorbed in their world and intent on their path, their shoulders suddenly bumped!

Neither was a professional attention payer, yet here they were—why here, why now, why them?

Madalyn's basket of pastries, ready for delivery, toppled to the ground in the collision. Jamie immediately went to pick them up as they bumped heads. Both laughed and apologized, filling the basket with the fallen pastries before heading on their way. But little did they know that fleeting moment had left a mark. That night, Jamie couldn't stop thinking about the lady's smile. He wished he had gotten her name.

Still, Jamie was a realist. A woman like that—both pretty and practical—was surely spoken for. Talking himself down from the fairytale-like accident, Jamie thought: *If this snow brought us together, maybe it could keep us together.* Then another question struck him—*Why is she walking to deliver pastries? Does she own a shop, or does she work for one?*

A few days passed, and reality had settled back in. Jamie was still stuck in this little town due to the snow. That morning, he went out to this quaint little pastry shop that the locals had told him served a great cup of coffee.

Sitting and sipping his regular cup of coffee, he scanned the shop, hoping to see his accidental princess. Instead, he found only locals, regulars who exchanged familiar nods and small talk. Jamie was a new face, so he drew attention, too. Then, just as he took his last sip, he looked up—and to his surprise, he saw something far beyond what he expected.

Madalyn walked through the door, her hands full of supplies for the business. That sweet smile he remembered as she greeted the locals and staff a good morning. He couldn't believe his eyes—finally, a second chance to get her name! A flurry of thoughts raced through his head as she put her apron on, getting ready to start her shift. Who was this woman? How could he possibly get her attention? Would she remember him?

Jamie acted instinctually and attempted to help her as she carried the supplies. He locked eyes with Madalyn in hopes she understood the situation at large. *I look at you, you look at me,* Jamie thought. However, he knew what the ingredients she carried would equate to, so locked in his thoughts, he became.

Madalyn thanked him and said, "Wait—you look familiar. Aren't you the out-of-towner I ran into last week? And here you are again, helping me with full hands." She smiled warmly. "My name is Madalyn. Welcome to my shop. What's your name?"

Jamie chuckled, brushing snow off his sleeve. "Name's Jamie. And now that I've run into you twice, I feel like I should at least buy a pastry or something."

Madalyn grinned. "Twice, huh? Must be fate—or just a tiny town." She shifted the weight of her bags. "I'm stocking up for a big town event. Snow Valley takes its sweets very seriously."

Jamie raised an eyebrow. "And you haul all this by yourself?"

"Small business owner perks." She smirked. "Now, your turn. What's keeping you in our little frozen paradise?

"Well, Madalyn, what brings me here is what keeps you here: warmth amongst cold and friendship. I'm finding my place in town and am beginning to love it. How long have you been here?

As Madalyn spoke, glee sparkled in her eyes. "This is my home. I was born and raised here—I still live in my childhood house. This town helped raise me."

As she talked to Jamie, neither realized that hours had passed as they talked and got to know each other.

A worker approached, hesitant but urgent. "I'm so sorry to interrupt, Madalyn, but a large order just came in—we need your help."

Madalyn turned to Jamie with a warm smile. "It was so lovely to meet you. I hope we can do this again."

Jamie couldn't stop thinking about Madalyn's radiant smile and how her eyes seemed to hold a thousand unspoken stories. He didn't know what drew him back to the pastry shop the following morning, but something more profound than curiosity nudged him there. Perhaps it was the snowstorm keeping him in town or the allure of a warm cup of coffee in a place that felt oddly comforting. Or perhaps... it was her.

The aroma of freshly baked pastries enveloped him as he walked through the shop's door. But today, the warmth seemed tinged with something off l, a tension in the air that hadn't been there before. The chatter of the locals was hushed, and the staff exchanged glances, their smiles faltering when they thought no one was looking.

Jamie scanned the room, his eyes finally landing on Madalyn. She was behind the counter, her back turned to him, seemingly distracted by something on her phone. Her shoulders were tense, and the bright energy she carried yesterday seemed dimmed.

"Morning, Miss Madalyn," Jamie said softly as he approached the counter.

She turned quickly, startled, but when she saw him, a small smile returned to her lips. "Jamie! You're back." Her voice was warm but nervous.

"I couldn't resist," Jamie replied, returning her smile. "But something feels different today. Is everything all right?"

Madalyn hesitated for a moment before sighing. "It's probably nothing," she said, lowering her voice and glancing toward the window. "Just... a feeling I can't shake. Someone's been hanging around the shop during the past few days. At first, I thought it was the snowstorm keeping people nearby, but now..." She trailed off, shaking her head. "Anyway, it's silly. I'm sure it's nothing; I just have a feeling."

Jamie frowned, his instincts kicking in. "You're not silly," he said, his voice steady. "If something feels off, trust that gut of yours. Do you want me to stick around for a while?"

Her smile softened. "I wouldn't want to keep you."

"Consider it me repaying you for the coffee," Jamie interrupted with a grin. "Besides, I've got nowhere else to be."

Madalyn couldn't put her finger on it, but something about Jamie brought her peace. She enjoyed his company.

Jamie sat at that counter while Madalyn worked as the day went on. Sharing witty conversations made the time pass quickly, and before they knew it, the day was done. Feeling grateful to Jamie for the day, Madalyn asked him if he would like to come over for a home-cooked meal to show her appreciation for his help. Jamie was elated.

"Of course, I'd love to!" he said. They closed the shop together and headed to Madalyn's house.

They walked together through the quiet, snow-covered streets. The air was crisp, and their breaths hung in clouds before them. Jamie couldn't help but feel like the town had softened since his arrival, the once unforgiving cold now carrying a sense of warmth.

As they approached Madalyn's house—a charming, snow-dusted home with twinkling lights— Jamie felt a pang of nostalgia. It reminded him of something he couldn't quite place, a warmth he hadn't felt in years.

Madalyn unlocked the door and gestured for him to come inside. "Make yourself comfortable," she said, slipping off her coat and heading toward the kitchen. "I'll get started on dinner."

The house was warm, contrasting to the frost biting at Jamie's skin. As he stepped inside, a familiar scent—cinnamon and something subtly floral—welcomed him.

Then, movement. A flicker of shadow at the edge of the tree line. Just a trick of the wind? His body tensed instinctively.

"Jamie?" Madalyn's voice was soft, her silhouette framed by firelight. "You, okay?"

He hesitated before plastering a grin on his face. "Yeah. Just admiring the view."

Jamie forced a smile, slipping off his coat, but his mind was elsewhere.

He knew that feeling.

The hair at the back of his neck stood on end—not just from the cold. How the shadow had moved, lingered, and waited wasn't just paranoia. Someone was watching them.

And Jamie had spent too much of his life being watched.

The house was cozy and inviting, filled with the smell of cinnamon and pine. Photos of Madalyn's family and the town adorned the walls, and a crackling fire warmed the living room. Jamie couldn't shake the sense of safety he felt here, but it was undercut by the unease that had been following him since the shop.

As Madalyn busied herself in the kitchen, Jamie offered to help, but she insisted he relax. He settled into a chair, the firelight casting flickering shadows around the room. His mind wandered back to the shadow he'd seen outside. Was it just his imagination, or was something or someone watching them?

Dinner was a hearty stew paired with freshly baked bread Madalyn had brought home from the shop. They laughed and talked, the warmth of their connection cutting through the cold unease that lingered in Jamie's mind.

But as the evening wore on, Jamie's instincts refused to be silenced. The faint sound of footsteps outside the window caught his attention. He glanced at Madalyn, blissfully unaware, recounting a story about the town's winter festival.

Jamie decided not to alarm her yet; he'd keep his guard up, just in case.

But suddenly, there was a knock at the door. Madalyn wondered who it could be at this hour. Jamie was right behind her as she went to get the door, checking to ensure everything was okay, especially after the lingering feeling of someone following her today.

When she opened the door, her eyes landed on a man with a briefcase. The man promptly said, "Hi, my name is

Greg, I'm with Kenshaw Holdings. I've been walking around your shop and other small businesses. My firm wants to propose a plan for the area to bring in new businesses and revenue. Is now a good time to talk?"

Madalyn's couldn't hide her startled expression. She wasn't expecting visitors, let alone a corporate representative at her doorstep. "I...uh...it's a little late for business meetings," she said, her voice tinged with apprehension.

Jamie's instincts flared again. Something about this man seemed off, though he couldn't quite put his finger on it. Kenshaw Holdings. The name felt familiar, tugging at a thread in Jamie's memory. He couldn't place where he'd heard it before, but a sense of unease crept over him. Greg pressed on, unfazed by Madalyn's hesitation. "I understand, Ms. Madalyn, but I think you'll find our proposal intriguing. We want to revitalize this area, create opportunities, and elevate the town's appeal. I took particular interest in your shop. It's the kind of unique charm that would benefit greatly from increased foot traffic."

Madalyn's fingers curled around the counter's edge, pressing white knuckles against the smooth wood. A scarce pulse ticked beneath her skin—too fast, too noticeable.

Jamie took a step closer, a quiet but deliberate move. "Now might not be the best time," he said, his voice even but edged with something firm. "If you leave some information, Madalyn can review it later."

Greg's eyes flicked toward Jamie. He paused, just for a second. A moment too long.

Then, he smiled. But it wasn't just a businessman's smile. It was the kind of grin a man gives when he knows something you don't want him to say out loud.

"Jamie, was it?" Greg's voice was too casual. "You look familiar."

Jamie's stomach clenched. He kept his expression neutral. "Don't think so."

Greg tilted his head, seeming amused. "You sure about that?" He tapped his fingers against his briefcase. "You ever spend time in Chicago? Because I could swear, we've crossed paths before."

Jamie kept his voice steady. "Not unless you vacation in the Everglades."

Greg chuckled, but his eyes didn't match his laughter. "Huh. Must be my mistake."

As the door closed, Madalyn let out a small sigh. "What was that all about?" she asked, clutching the envelope nervously.

Jamie shook his head. "I don't know, but something about him didn't sit right with me."

Later that night, while Madalyn was cleaning up from dinner, Jamie sat by the fire, turning the sleek black envelope over in his hands. Kenshaw Holdings. The name continued to nag at him. Could it be connected to the same corporation he'd run across during his last job? This company wasn't afraid to play dirty to get what it wanted.

Jamie's mind raced. If it was the same Kenshaw Holdings, Madalyn's quaint town might be in danger of losing its charm and something far worse.

Madalyn hummed softly to herself, tidying up the kitchen; Jamie sat on the couch with his phone in hand, the sleek black envelope from Kenshaw Holdings resting on the coffee table before him. His gut told him there was more to Greg's visit than meeting the eye. The name Kenshaw Holdings tugged at his memory like a stubborn thread, daring him to pull at it.

Jamie hesitated for a moment, glancing toward Madalyn in the kitchen. He didn't want to alarm her, not when the evening had been so warm and comforting. But he couldn't ignore the chill.

Had settled in his spine since Greg's departure. With a few swipes on his phone, he began his search. The results were overwhelmed by news articles on business acquisitions and corporate expansions. Kenshaw Holdings had a reputation for sweeping into small towns, buying out beloved businesses, and replacing them with cookie-cutter corporate ventures.

There were whispers of shady dealings, lawsuits quietly settled, and even claims of intimidation. His eyes narrowed as he scrolled through the articles. This wasn't just a development firm; this was a machine, and it didn't seem to care what or who it crushed in the process.

"Jamie?" Madalyn's voice broke his concentration. He quickly locked his phone and looked up to see her standing in the doorway, a curious smile on her face. "What are you up to over there?"

Jamie offered a casual smile, even as his mind raced. "Just scrolling through some emails. Nothing important."

Madalyn came over and sat next to him, the warmth of her presence momentarily easing his tension. She reached for the envelope on the table. "Do you think I should even look at this?"

Jamie placed a hand over hers, his voice steady but firm. "Not tonight. Let's take it slow, okay? We've got time to figure this out."

But Jamie knew they didn't have as much time as he'd just told her. If Kenshaw Holdings was involved, trouble wasn't far behind. And for reasons he couldn't yet explain, Jamie felt a fierce need to protect Madalyn and her town, even if it meant confronting shadows from his own.

"So, are you up for a meeting tomorrow to discuss this with me? I could use another set of eyes. Have you ever heard of Kenshaw before? I wonder what plans they have for the betterment of our community," Madalyn said, her voice brimming with hope. "New growth opportunities sound exciting!" she added, blissfully unaware of foul play. Madalyn had always been naïvely optimistic.

Jamie was quite the opposite—while Madalyn's head was in the clouds, Jamie's feet were firmly planted on the ground. A bad feeling gnawed at him about the entire situation. At that moment, he realized what had brought him to this small town and to meet this incredible woman. His mission became to uncover what was happening and help Madalyn and other small businesses resist the corruption he knew this new venture would bring.

As Jamie looked at Madalyn, her eyes full of hope and curiosity, he couldn't bring himself to share the storm of doubt inside him. Instead, he forced a smile. "I'll meet you tomorrow, Madalyn. We'll figure this out together."

She smiled brightly, her optimism lighting up the room. "Thank you, Jamie. I appreciate it."

Jamie's mind raced as they finished their wine and said their goodnights. He couldn't shake the feeling that Kenshaw Holdings was no stranger to him. He couldn't pinpoint why the name was a warning, but his instincts had never steered him wrong. If this company was

Anything like the ones he had dealt with in his past, the stakes for Madalyn and her town were higher than she could imagine.

The night was still as Jamie walked back to his inn. Snow crunched under his boots, and the cold air bit his cheeks. The once charming town now seemed cloaked in an eerie silence. He caught movement again out of the corner of his eye, and a shadow darted between the snow-laden trees. He turned quickly, but there was nothing there.

Paranoia? Maybe. But Jamie had learned long ago to trust his instincts. Someone was watching, and he was sure of that.

As Jamie trudged through the snow back to his inn, the weight of the black envelope felt heavier than it should have. He couldn't shake the tension that had followed him since Greg's visit. The inn's warmth was a welcome relief from the biting cold, but the questions swirling in Jamie's mind refused to settle.

Jamie sat at the desk, the envelope in front of him like a dare. He reached for his laptop, his fingers hesitating over the keys before typing, "Kenshaw Holdings scandals."

The search results made his stomach drop. Town after town had been promised revitalization, only to see their businesses stripped away and replaced with corporate chains. Lawsuits alleging fraud, coercion, and environmental violations piled up, each quietly settled before hitting trial.

He flipped through the documents in the envelope, his breath hitching as he found the fine print: a clause stating that properties would transfer outright to Kenshaw after five years. Worse, there was a confidentiality agreement prohibiting signees from speaking out.

Jamie leaned back in his chair, running a hand through his hair. "This isn't just business," he muttered. "It's a takeover."

The following day, Jamie arrived early at the pastry shop. Madalyn greeted him with a steaming cup of coffee and a warm smile. Still, the carefree air she carried yesterday had dimmed slightly. "I stayed up late thinking about the offer," she admitted, handing him the sleek black envelope. "It almost too good to be true." Jamie slid the packet across the table as Madalyn poured their coffee the following day. "We've got a problem," he said, his voice low. "Kershaw isn't what they seem. They're here to take over."

Jamie nodded, flipping through the packet of papers. His eyes skimmed over the glossy pages filled with promises of revitalization, increased revenue, and modern amenities. But the fine print caught his attention with clauses about eminent domain, buyouts, and profit shares that heavily favored Kershaw. The whole deal screamed exploitation.

"Did you notice this?" Jamie pointed out a line about the town's approval being overridden if a certain percentage of business owners signed on.

Madalyn frowned, leaning closer to read. "What does that mean?"

"It means," Jamie said, his voice tight, "they don't need everyone's agreement. There are just enough signatures to make it look legitimate. Once that happens, the rest of the town loses their say." He pushed the papers back toward her, his jaw clenched. "Madalyn, this isn't about helping the community. It's about taking it over."

Her face fell as realization dawned. "You think they're lying?" "I don't think so," Jamie replied. "I know."

Before they could dive more profoundly, the bell over the shop door jingled. Jamie's pulse quickened as Greg stepped inside, his sharp eyes scanning the room.

"Good morning," he said, his voice as smooth as the sheen on his briefcase. "I hope I'm not interrupting. I was just wondering if you had time to read over our proposal. A few of your fellow businesses have already agreed to this amazing opportunity for your small town. I just stopped by to see if you had any questions and if you would like to go ahead and sign before this opportunity passes your business by."

Madalyn, thinking about Jamie's words, felt a sudden wave of uneasiness. "I, um, I'm still looking these papers over. I don't think I'm quite ready to sign just yet. Could you give me a few more days? I'll reach out when I'm ready with my decision."

Greg was super sure that she would sign, of course. "Here's my card. Call me when you're ready, but don't wait too long, Madalyn." He grabbed a freshly baked scone as he walked out the door. Madalyn, now feeling the weight of this decision, looked to Jamie. What do we do? How do we save this town and the small businesses within it?

Jamie stood by the window, watching Greg's car disappear. He couldn't shake the feeling that this wasn't just a business deal but a calculated move. Kenshaw Holdings didn't just buy property. They took it, molded it, and left towns like Madalyn's unrecognizable. He'd seen it before, and it never ended well.

Madalyn sat at the kitchen table, nervously flipping through the sleek black packet Greg had left. "Jamie, do you think I'm overthinking this? I mean, his offer could bring new people to the town. That's good, isn't it?"

Jamie turned back to her, his eyes serious. "Madalyn, sometimes what looks good on paper is anything but. Kenshaw Holdings doesn't just bring new people—they bring control. Pushing them out will be almost impossible once they have a foothold. You could lose everything that makes this town and your shop special."

Madalyn frowned, her optimism dimming slightly under Jamie's words. "But how do we fight something like that? I'm just one person and... I don't know where to start."

Jamie pulled up a chair beside her. "We start by figuring out what they want. Deals like this don't happen out of the goodness of someone's heart. There's something here they're after, and we need to find out what it is."

He glanced back at the packet. "Can I take this and look it over tonight? There might be something in here they don't want you to see."

Madalyn nodded. "Of course. I trust you, Jamie."

Jamie pored over the documents in the packet as the evening wore on. At first glance, everything seemed above board: attractive offers, promises of economic growth, and testimonials from other towns that had supposedly thrived under Kenshaw Holdings' influence. But Jamie's gut told him there was more to it, something lurking beneath the glossy surface.

Then, he found a clause buried deep in the fine print. If Madalyn signed, Kenshaw Holdings wouldn't just lease part of her property; they'd own it outright after five years. Worse, the agreement gave them the right to redevelop the land at their discretion, with no input from the current owners.

Jamie's stomach churned. This wasn't an offer. It was a takeover.

He glanced at Madalyn, who had dozed off on the couch, her face peaceful despite the day's tension. Jamie couldn't let her lose everything she'd worked so hard for, and he couldn't stand the thought of her town being swallowed whole by corporate greed.

The following day, Jamie made some calls. He still had a few connections in the corporate world, people who owed him favors. If Kenshaw Holdings thought they could march into this town, they were in for a fight.

After talking with some old colleagues, Jamie realized everything he had thought about Kenshaw Holdings was true. They had done the same thing to a small town near his home.

Several of the people he spoke to said that if there was anything he needed to let them know, he should do so, but he should not let those businesses sign the contracts.

Jamie knew he needed a plan. He had spent the entire night deep in thought, barely sleeping. *How could he stop this from happening?* he wondered. *How could he get all these small business owners, entranced by the polished allure of such a fantastic deal, to see the reality of what was about to befall their beloved town?*

The following day, Jamie shared his concerns with Madalyn over coffee. The soft morning light filtered through the kitchen window, casting a warm glow that contrasted sharply with the cold, hard reality of the situation.

"Madalyn," Jamie began, his voice low but resolute, "we must warn the others. Kenshaw Holdings isn't just trying to revitalize this town—they're setting it up for a hostile takeover. If those contracts get signed, this place will never be the same."

Madalyn stirred her coffee absently; her brows furrowed in thought. "But how do we convince everyone? People are already excited about the promises Kenshaw's made. When Greg came by the shop yesterday he seemed so... sincere."

Jamie leaned forward, his gaze intense. "That's how they operate. They play on your hopes and dreams, turning them into leverage. I spoke with some people who've dealt with them before. Once Kenshaw gets their foot in the door, they'll gut this town for profit."

Madalyn's hands trembled slightly as she set her cup down. "What do we do?" she asked, her voice barely above a whisper.

Jamie's jaw tightened. "We need to show the truth. There's a pattern to their operations—false promises, corporate takeovers, and community displacement. If we can find evidence of what they've done before, we might be able to stop them here."

Madalyn nodded slowly, the weight of the situation pressing down on her. "I'll talk to the other business owners," she said. "Maybe if they hear it from me, they'll listen."

Jamie reached out and placed a reassuring hand on hers. "We'll do this together. I'm not letting this town fall without a fight."

The two spent the next few days gathering evidence, going from business to business, and talking to the locals about Kenshaw's false promises. The people were shocked; Greg seemed so lovely, and the offer even nicer. Could he be a wolf in sheep's clothing? The whole town was scared about what might come next for their quiet little town.

Could these small businesses be strong enough to keep this corporation out? What about those who had already signed? What now? The whole town was looking to Jamie and Madalyn for help.

Jamie and Madalyn sat in the corner booth of the town's only café, their table littered with notes, highlighted documents, and half-empty coffee cups. Jamie's jaw was set, eyes scanning the café door like a hawk. The evidence they'd uncovered was damning but presenting it to the town was another matter.

The bell above the door jingled, and Greg stepped inside. He wasn't alone. Two sharply dressed men flanked him, their presence screaming authority. The trio moved to the counter, but Greg's eyes immediately locked onto Jamie and Madalyn. With a practiced smile, he made his way to their table.

"Well, well," Greg said smoothly, his voice carrying a faint edge. "If it isn't my favorite business owner and her loyal... friend." His gaze flicked briefly to Jamie, his tone laced with condescension.

Jamie leaned back, forcing a calm he didn't feel. "Greg. What a surprise. Couldn't resist the coffee here?"

Greg chuckled, though it lacked warmth. "I find myself drawn to the charm of this town. I imagine that your business proposal has drawn you to ours." He gestured to the documents spread across the table. "Hard at work, I, see?"

Madalyn shifted uncomfortably, but Jamie kept his focus on Greg. "Just doing our homework," Jamie said evenly. "You know how it is—can't be too careful with big decisions."

Greg's smile faltered, just for a moment. "Of course. Due diligence is important. But I hope you're not overcomplicating things. This is a once-in-a-lifetime opportunity, after all."

Jamie tilted his head, his tone sharpening. "Funny you should say that. Kenshaw Holdings has habitually given 'once-in-a-lifetime opportunities' to small towns like this. What happens after those opportunities, though, isn't so charming."

Greg's eyes narrowed, his calm veneer cracking ever so slightly. "I'm not sure what you're implying, Mr. Jamie."

Jamie leaned forward, his voice low but firm. "I'm not implying anything. I'm stating a fact. We've seen the contracts. We've spoken to people from other towns Kenshaw's 'helped.' It's not revitalization; it's a *takeover.*"

Madalyn's hand brushed Jamie's under the table, a silent reminder to keep his cool. She turned to Greg, her voice steady but softer. "We've done much research, Greg. There are clauses in your contracts that would give Kenshaw total control over properties in just a few years. That's not what we signed up for."

As she spoke, Greg's smile turned cold. He sighed, rolling the briefcase handle between his fingers. "I lived in a town like this as a kid. Quiet. Safe. Dying."

Madalyn stiffened. "We're not dying."

Greg's smile was almost sad. "That's what we thought, too. Then, one day, we realized nostalgia doesn't pay the bills."

Jamie stood, his imposing presence overshadowing Greg's smooth demeanor. "I see a corporation preying on hardworking people and trying to take what isn't theirs. You can't bully this town into submission."

Greg straightened, his tone dropping to a dangerous calm. "Be careful, Mr. Jamie. People who dig too deep sometimes find themselves buried. And your past—well, not everyone might see you as the hero you're trying to play."

Madalyn gasped, but Jamie didn't flinch. He took a step closer to Greg, their faces mere inches apart. "My past isn't the problem here. You are. And this town isn't as easy a target as you think."

Greg gave a tight-lipped smile, then stepped back, adjusting his tie. "Enjoy your coffee. I'm sure we'll talk again soon." With that, he turned and left, his entourage trailing behind.

Jamie sat back down, his hands balled into fists. Madalyn reached for his arm, her eyes filled with worry. "Jamie, what did he mean about your past?"

Jamie sighed, running a hand through his hair. "It's a long story, and I'll tell you everything. But right now, we need to focus on saving this town."

Madalyn nodded, her trust in Jamie unwavering. "Whatever it is, we'll face it together."

As the café door closed behind Greg, Jamie couldn't shake the feeling that the real fight was beginning.

Madalyn said, "I've got it! Let's present this to the town hall. We'll show them all our evidence and get everyone on the same page. Let's gather the local businesses and government officials in one place to fight this together."

They worked diligently over the next few days, ensuring their case left no room for question. The local businesses and county officials would know Kenshaw's exact intentions.

They had an emergency hearing the following week and laid out all the facts. You could hear a pin drop; only the subtle gasp of disbelief could be heard. The town decided they were not going down without a fight. As a united force, they could not be stopped.

Madalyn's voice trembled with urgency. "We must act fast. Let's present this to the town hall— everyone must know the truth. We can't let Kenshaw ruin this town."

Jamie nodded, though his thoughts were clouded. "I agree, but Kershaw won't go down without a fight. We must be ready for whatever tricks they pull."

For the next few days, they buried themselves in work. Jamie couldn't shake the feeling that there was more to the story. Late one night, while Madalyn slept on the couch, he made a call to one of his old contacts in corporate law. The information he received was explosive—Greg wasn't just an agent for Kenshaw; he was also tied to shady deals with local officials. The contracts Kenshaw had already secured were riddled with illegal clauses, coercion, and under-the-table payoffs.

But that wasn't the worst of it. Jamie discovered that Greg had been targeting Madalyn specifically. Kenshaw's interest in Snow Valley wasn't just about the town; Madalyn's property sat on untapped land with significant mineral rights—rights that Kenshaw had already planned to seize.

Jamie debated whether to tell Madalyn. She was already under so much stress. But the following day, as they sipped coffee and reviewed their evidence, Jamie blurted it out.

Jamie sat at the edge of Madalyn's couch, laptop perched on his knees, the glow from the screen throwing deep shadows across his face. He had spent hours digging. And now, the truth sat before him like a loaded gun.

"Jamie?" Madalyn's voice was soft, hesitant. "What is it?"

He exhaled, rubbing a hand over his face before looking up. "They've been targeting you."

"What?"

"Your land, Madalyn." He tapped the screen, where an archived land survey flashed in bold letters. "There's mineral-rich land beneath your property. Kenshaw Holdings didn't just want to redevelop the town. They wanted your land and would take it, one way or another."

Silence stretched between them. Then, Madalyn's face slowly darkened, her hands curling into fists. "They think they can just—what? Bury me in contracts until I have no choice?"

Jamie's voice was low but firm. "Not if we stop them first. "Madalyn's face went pale. "My land? But... why? What are they after?"

"Mineral rights. Your property has significant value beyond what you know. Kenshaw planned to take everything—your shop, home, everything. They were going to bury you in debt and leave you with nothing."

Tears welled up in her eyes, but they didn't fall. Instead, anger flared. "They think they can take everything from me. From this town? Not a chance."

They worked tirelessly, investigating every lie Kenshaw had spun. After dedicating most of the evening to investigating Kenshaw's foul play, Jamie suddenly fell quiet for a reasonable time. Madalyn, although furious from what she found out about Kenshaw, became increasingly concerned about and focused on Jamie.

"Jamie?"

His name on her lips was soft, hesitant. Madalyn stood near the crackling fire, arms wrapped around herself—not from the cold, but from how quiet he'd been.

"Talk to me."

He wanted to. But some things weren't easy to say.

Finally, he exhaled, rubbing a hand down his face. "Greg knows me."

Madalyn frowned. "What?"

"Or at least, he knows my past." Jamie hesitated, then gestured toward the folder of documents they'd gathered against Kershaw. "I know their playbook because I used to work for companies just like them."

Madalyn blinked. "You—what?"

Jamie swallowed. Now or never.

"Before I came here, I was a corporate risk investigator." He ran a hand through his hair, staring into the fire. "It was my job to find 'problems'—the kind that get in the way of buyouts, mergers, hostile takeovers. I dug up dirt on people, their businesses, their personal lives—whatever the higher-ups needed to make them sign."

Madalyn took a slow step toward him, her voice careful. "So you—"

"I ruined people," Jamie admitted, his jaw tight. "Just like Greg is trying to ruin you."

Silence.

Finally, she spoke. "So why did you stop?"

Jamie let out a rough breath. "Because I finally saw what I was doing." He shook his head, eyes dark with memory. "The last town I worked on wasn't just numbers on a page. Real people lost everything because of a signature I helped force. One woman—she lost her home, her business. The place was bulldozed in under a week." His voice was quieter now. "She called me a monster."

Madalyn's breath hitched.

Jamie forced himself to look at her. "I left that world. But people like Greg? They don't forget. He knows who I am, and if he thinks he can use my past against me—"

Madalyn stepped closer. "He won't."

Jamie blinked.

She grabbed his hand, fingers warm against his cold skin. "You left that world behind. You're not that person anymore."

Jamie let out a breath. "What if I can't change what I did?"

"You already have."

When the day of the town hall arrived, Jamie and Madalyn were armed with damning evidence.

The town hall was packed, buzzing with tension. Snow Valley's future hung in the balance. Small business owners, families, and local officials filled every seat, murmuring anxiously as the meeting was about to begin.

At the front, Mayor Jenkins cleared his throat. "We're here to discuss the development proposal by Kenshaw Holdings." His gaze flicked toward Madalyn, who sat beside Jamie, the sleek black contract folder in her lap like a ticking bomb.

Before anyone else could speak, the doors slammed open.

Greg strode in, his tailored suit crisp, his smirk unreadable. He wasn't alone. Two men in corporate attire followed, their presence reeking of authority. A third man—a lawyer, Jamie guessed—clutched a briefcase.

Greg spread his hands, addressing the crowd like a politician at a rally. "Good evening, everyone. I know there's been much talk about our proposal. Misinformation, even. I'm here to set the record straight."

Jamie clenched his fists. *Here we go.*

Greg continued, his voice smooth, rehearsed. "Kenshaw Holdings isn't here to take anything from you. We're here to help. Imagine a snowy valley with thriving tourism, bustling restaurants, and a revitalized economy. That's what we're offering. Change is hard, I get that. But stagnation? That's worse."

Madalyn stood, her voice cutting through the room. "You mean like all the other towns you've 'helped'? The ones you left in ruins?"

Greg's smile tightened. "Ms. Madalyn, I understand your hesitation. But fear shouldn't stop progress."

Jamie slammed a document onto the table. "Neither should fraud."

Gasps rippled through the audience. Greg's smug expression faltered. "Excuse me?"

Jamie flipped open the file, his voice cold. "We did some digging. It turns out Kenshaw Holdings has a pattern that starts with friendly proposals and ends with hostile takeovers."

He pulled out photographs, financial records, and legal complaints from towns Kenshaw had wrecked. "Here's Maple Ridge. They signed your deal—and lost every local business within five years. Brookhaven? You promised a 'revitalization project'—that ended with mass evictions. Should I go on?"

The room erupted in whispers. People shifted uneasily, some glaring at Greg.

Greg's jaw tightened. "You're making baseless accusations, Mr. Jamie."

Jamie's smile was sharp. "You sure? Because we found your paper trail." He flipped another page, highlighting a buried clause in the Snow Valley contract. "This right here? It states that after five years, all properties under your 'development' fully own Kenshaw Holdings."

The crowd exploded.

"That's theft!"

"We'd lose everything!"

"You lied to us!"

Greg's calm veneer cracked. "Enough!" His voice boomed over the chaos. He turned to Mayor Jenkins. "This is ridiculous. This town needs us. And frankly, you don't have a better option."

Madalyn lifted her chin, her voice unwavering. "We do now."

Greg narrowed his eyes. "What?"

Madalyn pulled out a second folder. "After Jamie started investigating you, we reached out to other developers—ones who care about small towns."

She slid the folder across the table. Mayor Jenkins picked it up, his eyes scanning the pages. His eyebrows lifted, and then he smiled.

"This proposal," he said, holding it up, "is from a cooperative business group that prioritizes local ownership. It offers infrastructure funding without handing over control to a corporation."

Jamie leaned forward. "So, Greg, we have a better option."

The crowd roared in approval. People clapped, cheering for Madalyn and Jamie.

Greg's expression darkened, his fingers tightening into fists. He had lost.

But then—he played his last card.

Greg smirked, straightening his tie. "Well, well. Looks like you two did your homework. Impressive." He glanced at Jamie, his voice lowering. "But you, Mr. Jamie, might want to be careful."

Jamie's muscles tensed. "Is that a threat?"

Greg leaned in slightly, his smirk icy. "Just a warning. People who dig too deep tend to get buried."

Jamie didn't flinch. Instead, he leaned forward, his voice dangerously quiet.

"Funny thing about buried things, Greg. Eventually, someone digs them up."

A ripple of silence passed through the room. Greg's smirk faltered Jamie saw fear in his eyes for the first time.

Mayor Jenkins cleared his throat, standing tall. "Snow Valley has made its decision." He looked Greg dead in the eye. "Kenshaw Holdings is not welcome here."

The crowd erupted. Cheers. Applause. A few even started chanting Madalyn's name.

Greg's face twisted in barely restrained fury, but he had no choice. He turned on his heel and stormed out, his team scrambled after him.

Madalyn exhaled as the doors slammed shut, finally allowing a small, triumphant smile. She turned to Jamie.

"We did it."

Jamie grinned, shaking his head. "No. You did it."

Her eyes softened. "Couldn't have done it without you."

And just like that, Jamie realized something as the town celebrated around them.

He hadn't just saved the town.

He'd found something worth staying for.

Snow Valley – One Month Later

The snow had begun to melt, revealing the first hints of spring beneath the icy remnants of winter. The town had settled into a newfound rhythm—one free of Kenshaw Holdings' looming shadow.

Jamie sat on the porch of Madalyn's pastry shop; his fingers curled around a mug of steaming coffee. Across the street, townsfolk bustled about—not with worry, but with purpose. The community had taken its victory and turned it into action.

New signs hung in shop windows, a small business coalition had formed, and Snow Valley felt like home for the first time since Jamie arrived.

And it wasn't just the town that had changed.

Jamie looked toward the shop's entrance, where Madalyn leaned against the door frame, watching him.

She held two fresh croissants on a small plate, her apron dusted with flour. "You know, you're part of the furniture now," she teased.

Jamie smirked. "Yeah? I make a pretty good coffee-drinking, porch-sitting decoration."

Madalyn stepped closer, her voice quieter. "You know what I mean."

Jamie's heart did that stupid thing again—it felt too big for his chest when she looked at him like that.

Her hand brushed his as she set the plate down, the warmth of her fingertips lingering.

"I figured you'd be gone by now," she murmured, studying him. "Snow's melting. The roads are clear. The world's waiting for you again."

Jamie exhaled, shaking his head. "Funny thing about the world—it keeps spinning no matter where I stand. For once, I think I'd rather stay put."

Madalyn's lips parted slightly, a slow, knowing smile forming.

"You serious?" she asked.

Jamie leaned forward, resting his elbows on his knees. "I don't say things I don't mean."

Madalyn tilted her head, pretending to consider. "So, hypothetically, if I wanted to take you on a proper date—you know, without corporate sabotage and legal battles—"

Jamie chuckled. "I'd say it's about damn time."

She grinned, then took his coffee mug from his hand and replaced it with her fingers.

Jamie didn't resist.

Her skin was soft, warm, and genuine.

For months, he'd been moving, running, fighting, and surviving. He hadn't realized how much he needed a reason to stop.

And Madalyn? She wasn't just a reason. She was the reason.

She stepped closer, standing between his knees, looking down at him with that mischievous glint.

"So, is this the part where you kiss me?" she teased.

Jamie smirked. "Depends. Are you expecting some dramatic, movie-perfect moment?"

Madalyn sighed dramatically. "I mean, we fought corporate evil together. I think we deserve at least one cliché."

Jamie chuckled, shaking his head. "Fair enough."

Then, he pulled her down into his arms.

Madalyn's breath hitched—just for a second—before her lips found his, slow and sure.

And for the first time in years, Jamie felt grounded.

No more running. No more second-guessing.

Just her.

Just home.

But elsewhere...

Far away from Snow Valley, in a high-rise corporate office, Greg stood in front of a massive window, watching the city below.

His hands were clasped behind his back, his expression unreadable.

Behind him, a voice cut through the dimly lit room. "So... they refused?"

Greg didn't turn. "They did more than that. They exposed us."

A pause. Then, a slow, dry chuckle. "Well, we can't have that, can we?"

Greg's eyes narrowed. "No. We can't."

A brief silence filled the space before a file slid across the table.

Inside, photos of Jamie and Madalyn.

Notes on Jamie's past.

A single line at the bottom:

Phase Two: Contingency Plan Initiated.

The End.

Jamie and Madalyn will return in "Love & Lies: Heart of Cold".